This handbook contains top-secret documentation. Disclosure of its classified contents to a member of the Secret Kriminal Underground League, or any other anti-establishment party, constitutes a breach of the Official Secrets Act and carries a maximum life sentence.

Keep your handbook safe at all times. It can be simply disguised by slipping inside a nondescript book jacket – or, preferably, an anti-perception Chameleon Sleeve, available on request from M.I.9's Technical Development Department. Don't leave it in your locker. Or use it to prop up the wonky monitor in the school computer room.

DATA PROTECTION

Your handbook incl[...] [...]tion Chip and is printed on FastFlam[...] [...]iltration of M.I. High's intellig[...] [...]e remotely activated, causing [...] [...]y combust. The chip is also sens[...] [...]s of light – attempts to duplicate pages via photocopier or camera will similarly result in the handbook's self-destruction.*

* You might want to keep it away from your homework – just to be on the safe side.

PUFFIN BOOKS

Published by the Penguin Group
Penguin Books Ltd, 80 Strand, London WC2R ORL, England
Penguin Group (USA) Inc., 375 Hudson Street, New York, New York 10014, USA
Penguin Group (Canada), 90 Eglinton Avenue East, Suite 700, Toronto, Ontario, Canada M4P 2Y3
(a division of Pearson Penguin Canada Inc.)
Penguin Ireland, 25 St Stephen's Green, Dublin 2, Ireland (a division of Penguin Books Ltd)
Penguin Group (Australia), 250 Camberwell Road, Camberwell, Victoria 3124, Australia
(a division of Pearson Australia Group Pty Ltd)
Penguin Books India Pvt Ltd, 11 Community Centre, Panchsheel Park, New Delhi – 110 017, India
Penguin Group (NZ), 67 Apollo Drive, Rosedale, North Shore 0632, New Zealand
(a division of Pearson New Zealand Ltd)
Penguin Books (South Africa) (Pty) Ltd, 24 Sturdee Avenue, Rosebank, Johannesburg 2196,
South Africa

Penguin Books Ltd, Registered Offices: 80 Strand, London WC2R ORL, England

puffinbooks.com

First published in Puffin Books 2008
1

Copyright © Kudos Film & Television Limited, 2008
Photographs copyright © Kudos Film & Television Limited, 2008
Keith Brumpton created the Format for *M.I. High*. This book is
based on his original series concept and episodes.
BBC and the BBC logo are trademarks of the British Broadcasting Corporation
and are used under licence. BBC logo © BBC 1996.
Text written by Richard Dungworth

Set in Eurostile by Perfect Bound Ltd
Made and printed in England by Clays Ltd, St Ives plc

British Library Cataloguing in Publication Data
A CIP catalogue record for this book is available from the British Library

ISBN: 978-0-141-32363-3

The Official M.I. HIGH Spy Survival Handbook

Written by Richard Dungworth

PUFFIN

Books in the M.I. High series:

M.I. High: A New Generation

M.I. High: Secrets and Spies

The Official M.I. High Spy Survival Handbook

CONTENTS

Many congratulations on your acceptance to M.I. High – the leading military intelligence academy for fully fledged spies.

By joining the ranks of M.I.9's crack team of agents, you are embarking on a thrilling double-life as an undercover intelligence operative. You'll play a vital role in classified spy missions crucial to the security of your country. Something worth missing Chess Club for.

Since the formation of M.I.9, following the collapse of the established British Secret Services, this organization has done a great deal to combat crime and corruption in our society.

Nevertheless, the threat to British security is at an all-time high. The best efforts of the highly trained agents of M.I.9's adult division have so far failed to curb the activities of S.K.U.L., the nation's most dangerous criminal organization. Now, more than ever, we are turning to the talented young spies of our M.I. High division.

In response to increased enemy activity, I have directed that all M.I. High operatives be issued with this newly compiled survival handbook. The top-secret information within it has been contributed by a selection of our very best agents. The classified factfiles and tutorials included will equip you for the continuing struggle against the elusive Grand Master and the many other enemies of national security. And there are some top tips on hair and fashion too.

Study the handbook well. Keep its secrets secure.

And remember – trust no one.

SECTION ONE:
WELCOME TO
M.I. HIGH

COMPILED BY LENNY BICKNALL

'Joining M.I. High is the beginning of a remarkable adventure. As an M.I.9 agent, you'll have the opportunity to live out an action-hero lifestyle most schoolchildren only dream of. I remember my own early missions, alongside my old chums Chuckers and Ginger, the jolly japes we had . . . ahem . . . anyway . . . this introductory section includes all the background information you'll need as a new M.I. High recruit.'

THE OLD-SCHOOL SPIES

The origins of the British Secret Intelligence Service – the SIS – go back over a hundred years. By the early part of the twenty-first century, the organization had become outdated and ineffective. With several of its key operations centres infiltrated, and many of its best undercover agents retired or rumbled, the Secret Intelligence Service could no longer operate effectively.

It was time for a major shake-up. The fast-moving twenty-first-century world demanded a brand-new generation of spies – young, dynamic and in touch with today's technology.

A NEW APPROACH

The SIS responded to the crisis in its old-style organization by setting up a new division of M.I.9. Its brief was to reinvent the modes and methods of espionage to tackle the contemporary criminal underworld. As part of its innovative approach, it adopted a radical recruitment policy – children were included among its newly enlisted agents. Their role was to be M.I.9's best-kept secret.

M.I.9 TODAY

Today, the enemies of the state are more numerous, devious and difficult to apprehend than ever before. But while they focus their evil attention on the main M.I.9 headquarters and the activities of its adult operatives, they little suspect that many of the Intelligence Service's most dangerous missions are being undertaken by an elite team of teenage agents, operating out of state-of-the-art headquarters, concealed in a place no one would ever think to look.

On the surface, St Hope's School is a typical inner-city comprehensive. Like many, it has a bungling headmaster, a staff boasting a wide variety of personality disorders, pupils ranging from delightful to delinquent, and a canteen that serves gravy and custard which are hard to tell apart.

But beneath its ordinary exterior, St Hope's hides a secret of national importance. Its pupils include an elite team of Secret Service agents – Daisy Millar, Blane Whittaker and Rose Gupta – who are permanently on standby to carry out undercover missions at the direction of M.I.9.

SPIES

St Hope's is the base for M.I. High, the top-secret headquarters from which you, as a new M.I.9 agent, will operate. Although you might want to bring a packed lunch.

DON'T BLOW IT

To succeed in your intelligence role, you'll need to blend in with the ordinary pupils at St Hope's. If you blow your own cover, or give away the true identity of any of your fellow agents, M.I.9's mission to combat organized crime will be seriously compromised. Even your closest friends and family must know nothing of your top-secret double-identity.

KEY CONTACT

You and your fellow spies are not alone at St Hope's. The school's personnel includes one adult M.I.9 operative. This individual will be your link with M.I.9 Head Office, overseeing your continuing training and intelligence activities. This key contact, working under deep cover as the school's caretaker, is agent Lenny Bicknall.

Name: Leonard Bicknall

Age: Undisclosed. Older than he likes to admit.

Background
A long-serving M.I.9 agent, with an impressive record of exposing and neutralizing enemy activity.

Cover identity
- Poses as the school caretaker at St Hope's.
- To keep a low profile, he adopts a meek, unassuming manner, allowing Mr Kenneth Flatley (Headmaster of St Hope's) to push him around.
- Wears scruffy overalls and a woolly hat.

Role within M.I.9

> Responsible for overseeing the M.I. High team.
> Liaises with Head Office in order to brief his agents at the outset of each assignment. Reports directly to the Head of M.I.9 and, when necessary, the Prime Minister, to update them on mission progress.
> Wears a sharp suit and snazzy tie.

Additional data

> During his years of active service, worked closely with Agent Charles 'Chuckers' Chuckworth and Agent Roderick 'Ginger' Rogers.
> Has a soft spot for Ms Helen Templeman – his agents' form teacher.

Performance assessment

HIGHS:

> Personally instructed Carla Terrini, five times winner of the Young Spy of the Year Award.
> Solely responsible for training the current outstanding M.I. High team.

LOWS:

> Kept his own M.I. High team in the dark while trying to outmanoeuvre Terrini and her Air One unit.
> Has a tendency to reminisce and ramble on about his 'glory days' in the field.
> His sense of humour is terrible and not to be encouraged.

CENTRE OF OPERATIONS: M.I. HIGH HQ

At first glance, St Hope's doesn't have much to offer as the headquarters of a key division of the nation's top intelligence agency. The classrooms are anything but hi-tech, and even the computer room has only one functioning PC – a prehistoric model with an ancient processor and minimal memory. But look below the surface – literally – and it's a very different story . . .

GOING UNDERGROUND

Far below the foundations of the school buildings lies a secret subterranean bunker purpose-built by M.I.9 to serve as the centre of operations for their junior division. It is equipped with an impressive range of cutting-edge technology – the very latest in computerized surveillance and intelligence systems, alongside a sophisticated analytical laboratory. The site itself is shielded from enemy detection by a state-of-the-art cloaking system. To all intents and purposes, this place doesn't exist.

LENNY'S LIFT

Access to the underground M.I. High command centre is by one means only – a top-secret express elevator hidden in one of the school corridors above. The secret lift is disguised as the caretaker's storeroom. A light switch just outside the door conceals a biometric lock. Only when this lock's scanner registers an authorized thumbprint will it allow entry to the storeroom.

ALL CHANGE

Once activated – by the operation of a lever concealed as a mop handle – the storeroom lift plummets at breakneck speed to the subterranean headquarters far below. But this is no ordinary express elevator. It incorporates M.I.9's groundbreaking GearChange technology – an astonishing system that automatically reclothes the agent in transit.*
An individual entering the storeroom in everyday school uniform steps out into the divisional headquarters seconds later, fully kitted out in their official M.I.9 attire.

* Despite setbacks with early GearChange prototypes – trousers failing to materialize, clothing being applied inside out, etc. – the current system appears fault-free.

SPY TIME

In the lulls between M.I.9 assignments, it's important that you engage fully in everyday school activities to maintain your cover and avoid arousing suspicion. But whether you are struggling to stay awake in history class, trying to find your PE kit or playing 'identify the vegetable' in the school canteen, it is vital that you are constantly on standby to respond rapidly when the call to action comes.

AGENT ALERT

All M.I. High agents are issued with a sophisticated two-way communicator disguised as an ordinary eraser-topped pencil. Carry this with you at all times. Should the need arise for Agent Bicknall to summon you, your pencil's 'eraser' – in reality a remote-activated LED (light-emitting diode) – will flash repeatedly. Before it draws unwanted attention, conceal or deactivate the alert beacon swiftly and make your way to headquarters immediately.

EXCUSE ME

In order that your sudden departure from the classroom doesn't arouse suspicion, you'll have to come up with a reason why you need to be excused. A list of suggested exit strategies is provided on page 86 of the handbook. If you prefer to invent your own, try to avoid the commonplace ('I need the loo') or the downright implausible ('I have an appointment with the President of the US').

MEET THE TEAM

In the case of an alert, all agents should rendezvous outside the caretaker's storeroom, then proceed as a unit to the underground headquarters. As the most recently appointed M.I. High member, you'll be joining an existing team of three top-flight teenage agents, who have together successfully carried out a significant number of challenging M.I.9 assignments. The operatives with whom you'll be sharing this lift are Agents Gupta, Whittaker and Millar.

AGENT PROFILE

Name: **Rose Gupta**

Age: 13 ¼

Background
) The eldest of three siblings.
) Her parents own the local DVD rental store.
) Her dad is very pushy, expecting A-grades across all her schoolwork.

Cover identity
) Year 9 pupil at St Hope's.
) She's the star academic performer of Ms Templeman's form, with a reputation among her more trendy classmates for being far too brainy and not very cool.
) The only pupil to wear her maroon and yellow St Hope's uniform strictly as requested, without accessorizing.

Role within M.I.9

❭ Her phenomenal IQ and scientific knowledge make her the thinking force of the M.I. High team.

❭ She's the technical and analytical expert, equally at home operating the hi-tech M.I.9 computer systems or state-of-the-art laboratory equipment.

Additional data

❭ Plays the clarinet (brilliantly) and tuba (very badly).

❭ Has a crush on Stewart Critchley, the geeky best friend of fellow M.I. High agent Blane Whittaker.

Performance assessment

HIGHS:

❭ Offered a place at the training academy of the CIA – the USA's Secret Intelligence Service – following her key role in exposing a double-agent within the American organization.

LOWS:

❭ Suffers whenever she needs to come up with an excuse to leave class, as her fellow agents always get in first. Repeatedly forced to fall back on the uninspired 'I need the toilet' exit strategy.

AGENT PROFILE

Name: **Blane Whittaker**

Age: 13 ¾

Background

❯ Parents divorced – lives with his mum.
❯ Has an elder brother, Kyle, who serves as a commando in the army.

Cover identity

❯ Like Agents Gupta and Millar, Blane is a pupil at St Hope's, in Ms Templeman's Year 9 form.
❯ He hangs out with Stewart Critchley, with whom he has been friends since the age of six.
❯ His grades aren't all they might be, but he's well-liked and good at sports.

Role within M.I.9

❭ Blane is the M.I. High team's lethal weapon – a martial arts prodigy with awesome hand-eye coordination and a black belt in karate.

❭ His peak physical condition means he is ideally suited to any aspects of a mission that require speed, agility or endurance.

Additional data

❭ Martial arts expert in many disciplines including the extremely difficult 'Slow Breath Panda'.

❭ Loves watching martial arts movies in order to learn the wisdom of the Kung Fu Masters – as well as watching some great action stunts.

Performance assessment
HIGHS:

❭ Helped prevent the sabotage of a UK space launch – and the likely injury or death of his brother – by taking out the nerdy computer hacker known as The Worm.

LOWS:

❭ Reading up on counter-surveillance while on the job, he lost track of fellow agent Daisy, whom he was supposed to be backing up.

❭ Botched a straightforward briefcase exchange with a CIA associate.

AGENT PROFILE

Name: **Daisy Millar**

Age: 13 ½

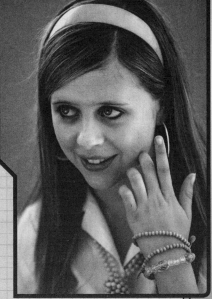

Background

> The only child of very wealthy parents, both of whom frequently work abroad.

> Her family have their own country estate and may have recently separated.

> At school, Daisy keeps her private life private.

Cover identity

> One of St Hope's in-crowd.

> She and friends Kaleigh and Zara are the trendsetting girls in Ms Templeman's class, more bothered about looking fabulous and fashionable than getting top grades.

Role within M.I.9

❯ A genius of disguise and deception. When an M.I. High mission calls for someone to adopt a fake persona – for purposes of infiltration, for instance – Daisy's extraordinary chameleonic ability to assume any role makes her first choice for the job.

Additional data

❯ Has a love-hate relationship with Blane Whittaker. Also had a crush on CIA agent Chad Turner and an infatuation with the heart-throb singers of boy-band Crush.

Performance assessment

HIGHS:

❯ Single-handedly exposed Sonya Frost's role in a S.K.U.L.-financed bid to plunge the Earth into a new ice age.

LOWS:

❯ Nearly cut fellow M.I. High agent Blane in half by being careless with her state-of-the-art Lipstick Laser gadget.

AGENT PROFILE

Name:

Age:

Background
)

AFFIX OFFICIAL M.I.9 IDENTITY HOLOGRAM HERE

Cover identity
)

Role within M.I.9

❯

Additional data

❯

Skills and specializations*

❯

* If you have any notable skills – perhaps you are a whizz at
electronics, have a photographic memory, or can speak eleven
languages – list them here.

PUBLIC ENEMY NUMBER ONE: S.K.U.L.

As an M.I.9 agent, you must be prepared for danger to come from any quarter. But by far the greatest and most persistent threat to the twenty-first-century world comes from the Secret Kriminal Underground League – S.K.U.L. This corrupt organization comprises an unknown number of affiliated villains who share a single sinister purpose – to create international chaos and havoc, for personal or political gain.

THE GRAND MASTER

S.K.U.L.'s despicable schemes are coordinated and overseen by a single enigmatic figure – the Grand Master. The true identity, appearance and whereabouts of this criminal mastermind remain unknown. Some useful data has, however, been collected by our agents in the field:

AGENT ZERO

Information recently gathered by M.I.9 suggests that in addition to his mob of hired hoodlums, the Grand Master has a reluctant protégé, codenamed Agent Zero, whom he is priming for a lead role in S.K.U.L.'s criminal future.

From the transcriptions of several intercepted telephone conversations, M.I.9 has drawn up a profile of Agent Zero. His repeated reference to the

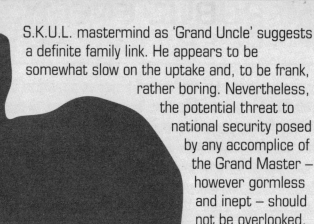

S.K.U.L. mastermind as 'Grand Uncle' suggests a definite family link. He appears to be somewhat slow on the uptake and, to be frank, rather boring. Nevertheless, the potential threat to national security posed by any accomplice of the Grand Master – however gormless and inept – should not be overlooked.

FELON FACTFILE

Name: Grand Master
Age: late fifties/early sixties, though this could of course be a disguise.
Appearance: grey hair, facial features unknown, wears a skull ring on fourth finger of right hand.
Companion: pet white rabbit called General Flopsy, who is his only known confidant.
Known accomplices: The Guinea Pig; Sonya Frost; CIA Agent Chad Turner; Silas Fenton; Vanessa Zeitgeist; his nephew, Agent Zero.
Location: Unknown; believed to use a hidden bunker somewhere on the floor of the Indian Ocean. Occasionally rents premises in North Wales.

EMERGENCY PROTOCOLS

The secrecy of M.I. High's activities is absolute and fundamental to its role. If compromised in any way, the unit could not continue to operate. As a consequence, emergency procedures are in place to cover all situations in which this secrecy may fall into jeopardy.

CODE RED

Code Red status signifies that hostile elements are on the verge of discovering the identity of an M.I. High agent or agents, or deducing St Hope's role as a centre of covert operations. In other words, our cover is about to be blown. In response to a Code Red, agents should immediately cease all intelligence activities and revert to their school-pupil cover persona.

Any incriminating personal equipment that does not auto-destruct – Pencil Communicators, explosive cosmetics, etc. – should be discreetly placed in the yellow swingbin provided outside the caretaker's storeroom. This will incorporate a silent, residue-free electromagnetic disintegrator. No school reports, thank you.

Should the crisis pass, agents will be personally informed and re-equipped by Spymaster Bicknall, and may resume normal activities.

ONLINE ASSAULT

M.I.9's computer systems have the most advanced firewall and anti-virus systems in existence. Nevertheless, remote infiltration by a hacker or bug remains a possibility. Should you suspect such activity, immediately launch the system's

HackBack application. This will prevent further data corruption and send out sophisticated web-crawlers to trace the culprit. Just don't pull the plug out.

HQ LOCKDOWN

In the event of actual physical infiltration of the underground M.I. High headquarters, one of several alarm systems operating within HQ will trigger 'lockdown' – the complete sealing off of the area and total system shut-down. This will contain the intruder or intruders and prevent access to agency data.

On receiving the lockdown alert, all operatives should report immediately to Agent Bicknall. He alone holds the authorization codes necessary to reactivate the M.I. High lift, and will supervise the team in apprehending any uninvited visitors.

COMPILED BY: Agent Millar

CASE NAME: The Sinister Prime Minister

ASSIGNMENT BRIEFING

Our first real mission – at last! Lenny told us M.I.9 was
concerned that our previously peace-loving Prime Minister
was suddenly acting out of character – all tough and
aggressive, like he was keen to start World War Three.
Lenny set up a ministerial visit to St Hope's so we could
check the PM out.

ACTION LOG

I went undercover as Charlotte Graham, a journalist, so that
I could get up close to the PM. He wasn't himself all right –
Rose ran DNA tests on the sample of his dandruff (gross)

I swiped and found out we were dealing with a **cyber-clone** of the real man. Blane and I tried to keep him busy to prevent him from declaring war on Europe, while Rose tracked the robot's control signal to a secret lab. Turned out it had been developed by some crackpot scientist calling herself The Guinea Pig, working for the Grand Master of course. Rose managed to neutralize her, and take control of the fake PM, so that he gave a speech promoting peace, rather then declaring war. Not bad for someone with such frumpy shoes . . .

GADGET PERFORMANCE NOTES
The Lipstick Laser worked a treat – let me cut my way out of a tight spot after Blane had made a **terrific** job (not) of backing me up.

MISSION RESULT:
CONSPIRACY FOILED

FELON FACTFILE
NAME: Professor Sally Moreau
ALIASES: The Guinea Pig
DETAILS: Brilliant but deranged scientist infamous for her unethical and discredited experiments. Self-experimentation has left her physically deformed – she has the snout and facial hair of a rodent. Fully signed-up member of S.K.U.L.
CURRENT STATUS: Incarcerated

COMPILED BY: *Agent Gupta*
CASE NAME: *Eyes on Their Stars*

ASSIGNMENT BRIEFING

Weird briefing – something was causing teenagers around the country to turn into zombies! Hundreds of zonked-out victims were raiding music stores, stealing CDs. M.I.9 wanted us to find out what was behind the zombie phenomenon, before it spread.

ACTION LOG

From CCTV footage of one music-store raid, we quickly figured out that the freaky teen behaviour was linked to airhead boy-band Crush. Daisy was all 'Oh, it can't be **them**!' – she's infatuated. When we managed to divert their tour bus to St Hope's, she was **desperate** to be the one to get up-close-and-personal with them – and then **fainted**! Very professional. Meanwhile, Blane and I dug up some web stuff about the band's manager, Tony Frisco. Turned out he was a wannabe pop singer himself, who'd been humiliated on a TV talent contest.

Daisy eventually managed to transmit some pics of the band's song lyrics, written by Frisco, back to HQ. I analysed them to find a subliminal, hypnotic message hidden in the lyrics. Frisco was brainwashing audiences to buy the Crush CD as part of a fanatic plan to have a global number one – and go on to control the entire musical world! Blane soon put him out of action, while I got working on an antidote song to reverse the hypnosis.

Meanwhile, Crush
had zombified
St Hope's and I had to sing the antidote song in front of
the whole school (cringe). Actually, it felt pretty good!

GADGET PERFORMANCE NOTES

The miniature camera in Daisy's false nails worked a treat.
And according to the style queen herself, the nails were the
'right shade' apparently.
(Good grief . . .)

MISSION RESULT:

CRISIS RESOLVED

FELON FACTFILE

NAME: Tony Frisco
ALIASES: None. Likes to think of
himself as 'The Boogieman'.
DETAILS: As a young man, achieved the lowest
score ever for his atrocious pop performance on
reality TV show *Pop Factor*. His public humiliation
fuelled a fanatical desire to achieve musical
domination through whatever means necessary.
CURRENT STATUS: Incarcerated

SECTION TWO:
THE SCIENCE OF SPYING

COMPILED BY AGENT ROSE GUPTA

'Science is cool. And it's vital in your role as a spy. In today's hi-tech world, being an effective force against organized crime means having at least one member of your team who can apply the principals of science, and scientific techniques, during assignments. At M.I. High, that's where I come in.'

M.I. HIGH-TECH

To make a first-class forensic scientist – someone who uses science in crime-busting – you'll need access to up-to-the-minute technology and equipment. At M.I. High, you're guaranteed just that. Our secret subterranean HQ includes a fully appointed scientific laboratory, and the latest-generation computer system, remotely linked to M.I.9's ultra-powerful server.

INFO-NET

Three large, top-spec plasma screens provide your main window on the digital world. M.I.9's specialized browser and search engine software, running on a state-of-the-art hardware platform, can quickly filter useful data from the web. Or you can access the agency's own top-secret intranet, to research suspects and follow up leads during an investigation.

EYES IN THE SKIES

Direct feeds to the HQ computer system from over a dozen separate spy satellites give you unrivalled remote surveillance capabilities too. Should you need to find out what the Lebanese Minister for Sport puts on his bird table, without leaving your (ultra-comfy) chair,* you have the necessary technology at your disposal.

KNOW YOUR STUFF

All the fancy techno-kit in the world won't help if you don't have the scientific know-how to go with it. A sharp scientific mind is the ultimate tool during any investigation. Work hard to build up your scientific knowledge – from plant biology to particle physics – and you'll soon find that you're spotting vital clues and cracking complex cases.

The following pages look at how the different branches of science can serve you as a spy – and how they might be used against you by your enemies.

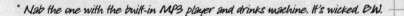

* Nab the one with the built-in MP3 player and drinks machine. It's wicked. DW.

SPY SCIENCES: BIOLOGY

Biology is the science of living things – and it's alive with applications in the world of espionage . . .

BIOMETRICS

However hard a villain tries to conceal their identity, they have some physical characteristics which, if you can detect them, will give them away. Fingerprints are one 'biometric' example – the pattern of ridges in the skin on a person's fingers is unique. Other biological signatures include patterns within the iris and retina of your eye, and even the exact configuration of your teeth.

M.I.9 has compiled a vast computer database of biometric data which you can check against evidence to identify a bad guy.

SCIENCE IN ACTION: BIOMETRIC LOCK

▶ The secret entrance to the M.I. High HQ – Lenny's storeroom – is protected by a biometric lock which recognizes the thumbprints of authorized agents.

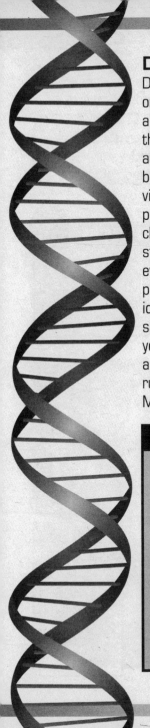

DNA

Deoxyribonucleic acid – or DNA for short – is a microscopic molecule that is found in almost all cells of the human body. From your point of view, as a spy, it has one particularly interesting characteristic – its exact structure is unique in every individual. No two people – unless they're identical twins – have the same DNA. If you can get your hands on any biological matter from a suspect – a hair, a fingernail – you can run a DNA profile and check it against M.I.9's database records.

GADGET SPEC: DNA SCANNER

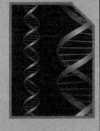

❯ A sophisticated DNA profiling device, disguised as a reporter's notebook. Daisy used it to test a sample of dandruff taken from the British Prime Minister who was behaving suspiciously. Analysis back at HQ revealed that the dodgy PM was actually a cyber-clone impostor!

SPY PSYCHOLOGY

Criminals may use one of several techniques – hypnosis, for instance – to influence or affect the minds of others. Mind control may sound like one of Stewart Critchley's wacko theories, but it's a genuine threat. A grasp of basic psychology – how the human brain works – is useful in detecting and dealing with the menace of mental manipulation.

SCIENCE IN ACTION: SUBLIMINAL MESSAGING

❯ When the teenage population began behaving like zombies, it took psychological know-how to work out why. The lyrics of a hit song had been cleverly devised to carry a hidden or 'subliminal' message, which hypnotized its listeners.

INVISIBLE EVIDENCE

Sometimes the smallest things make a big difference. It's vital not to overlook evidence that may not be visible to the naked eye. Biological clues can often be microscopic – a tiny pollen granule from a specific species of plant, stuck to a suspect's clothing, might be enough to confirm he was present at a crime scene.

TECH SPEC: SCANNING ELECTRON MICROSCOPE (SEM)

❯ A sophisticated microscope that can magnify objects up to 150,000 times. The SEM in the M.I. High lab will help you examine evidence for microscopic clues.

SIGNS OF STRESS

Be aware of the biological signs of stress – raised skin temperature, altered breathing pattern, increased heart rate and blood pressure. These telltale symptoms often reveal when a suspect is being dishonest with you.* Being able to control such symptoms yourself is crucial when you're working undercover.

TECH SPEC: POLYGRAPH ('LIE DETECTOR')

❯ A machine that reads a suspect's biological signs to detect whether they are telling the truth. As an M.I. High agent, you'll be trained to cheat a polygraphic test by overriding your vital signs.

* Or, if you're Daisy, it could just be the 'Chad Turner Effect'. D.W.

SPY SCIENCES: CHEMISTRY

Chemistry is the study of the properties of different substances and the ways in which they combine and react. As a spy, it can help you deal with anything from explosives to invisible inks.

CHEMICAL CLUES

A detailed chemical analysis of physical evidence can yield vital clues. Analysing traces of hand cream on a ransom note, for instance, might reveal a brand of cosmetics only sold through one outlet, hence narrowing the field of suspects.

TECH SPEC: GAS CHROMATOGRAPH

❯ A device used to profile the exact chemical components of a test substance. The chromatograph in the M.I. High lab will help you determine the chemical make-up of anything from a mystery drug to school canteen soup.

TOXICOLOGY

Members of S.K.U.L., and other international criminals, often turn to chemical agents to assist their sinister schemes. A knowledge of poisons (known as toxicology) is particularly valuable in the fight against crime.

Some formulae can even prove helpful during an undercover mission – a sleep-inducing sedative, for instance, might be one way past an overenthusiastic guard dog or sentry.*

SCIENCE IN ACTION: URGENT ANTIDOTES

❭ Several recent agency assignments have called for a chemical solution. In one instance, scientists at NOSE – the National Organization of Scientific Exploration – were poisoned with a 'regression formula' that made them behave like toddlers. In another, several individuals at St Hope's were affected by a mysterious truth serum. The answer in both cases was a chemical antidote, calculated and cooked up in our underground M.I. High lab.

* Or help you get through double history with Flatley. D.W.

SPY SCIENCES: PHYSICS

Physics is the study of the way things work – from solar systems to micromachines. But to M.I.9 agents and their criminal adversaries it means one thing only – gadgets.

DOOMSDAY DEVICES

Devising dastardly gadgets with which to hold the world to ransom is a favourite pastime of evil egomaniacs. And lurking behind each sinister scheme is usually a brilliant physicist. An example is the Grand Master's recent plot to plunge the Earth into an ice age using a climate-control machine – developed by Oxford-educated physicist Sonya Frost.

In the light of such enemy activity, it is vital that agents have a good grasp of advanced physics, in order to understand and undermine techno-terrorism.

SCIENCE IN ACTION: MISSILE MAYHEM

❯ When barmy army general Ryan Scarp seized remote-control of Europe's fully armed nuclear missiles, it was only the genius of child physicist Dylan Towzer – in the form of his Remote Missile Disarmer – that saved the day.

THE GADGET FACTORY

The super-smart scientists of M.I.9's Technical Development Department apply their knowledge of physics to devise new gadgets for use in the field – anything from oxygen-releasing gum, which enables an agent to breathe underwater, to a fake dental filling that works as a two-way radio.

A range of devices has been specifically developed to blend in with everyday school equipment, for use by young agents. Here are a handful of the hi-tech devices you'll have at your disposal as an M.I. High operative.

GADGET SPEC: LIPSTICK LASER
> A powerful laser designed to fit within an ordinary tubular cosmetic casing.
> Can cut a hole in metal at 10m.
> Available in Scarlet Gloss or Satin Rose.

GADGET SPEC: NAIL-CAM
> A set of fashionable false nails, one of which conceals a miniature camera capable of taking and transmitting high-definition digital images.

GADGET SPEC: THERMAL YO-YO
> A seemingly ordinary, fully functional toy.
> Twisting its separate halves causes it to radiate a thermal energy shield, which can protect an individual from sub-zero temperatures.

GADGET SPEC: SONIC DETONATOR

❭ A commonplace pin-on badge in a variety of designs.
❭ When activated, can blow a large hole in most substances.
❭ Wear with caution.

GADGET SPEC: PENCIL COMMUNICATOR

❭ Standard M.I. High issue.
❭ Incorporates an agent alert beacon – the eraser – and a two-way communicator.
❭ A transponder within the device can also be remotely activated to allow individual tracking.
❭ Do not sharpen.

GADGET SPEC: CALCULATOR CODE-BREAKER

❭ Looks like a standard calculator, but actually functions as a sophisticated code-breaker.
❭ Ideal for safe-cracking. Less so for maths class.

GADGET SPEC: FORCE-FIELD PODS

❭ Fake traffic bollards, designed to emit an invisible force field linking one pod to the next.
❭ Can be used to cordon off a high-security investigation site.

NEW EQUIPMENT PROPOSALS

During your M.I.9 missions, it's likely that there will be times when you wish you had a particular device to get you out of a tricky situation. Many existing M.I. High gadgets were inspired by an agent's experience in the field.

Any suggestions for new 'covert equipment' (more commonly known as gadgets) should be submitted to the Technical Development Department, following the example below. A brief description of the proposed device's purpose, and a rough sketch of its basic design, is all that's required – TDD will work out the technical details.

EQUIPMENT PROPOSAL FORM

EPF/002/078E

Please submit completed specification to the Technical Development Department.

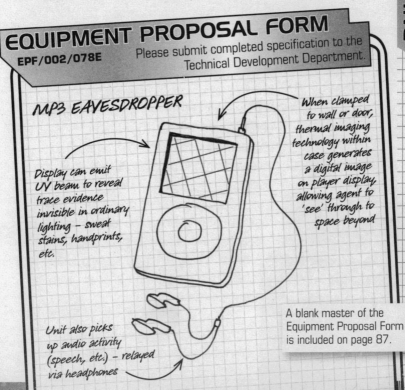

MP3 EAVESDROPPER

When clamped to wall or door, thermal imaging technology within case generates a digital image on player display, allowing agent to 'see' through to space beyond

Display can emit UV beam to reveal trace evidence invisible in ordinary lighting – sweat stains, handprints, etc.

Unit also picks up audio activity (speech, etc.) – relayed via headphones

A blank master of the Equipment Proposal Form is included on page 87.

MISSION FILE 3

COMPILED BY: *Agent Whittaker*

CASE NAME: *The Big Freeze*

ASSIGNMENT BRIEFING

Lenny told us that the weather was going crazy. (Like we hadn't noticed – it was **well** cold!) M.I.9 reckoned it was down to someone at the Weather Bureau carrying out unauthorized climate-control experiments (not a government conspiracy, like my mate Stewart thought). Our assignment was to infiltrate the Bureau and find out more.

ACTION LOG

To help get us in, Lenny set up a school field trip to the Weather Bureau. Rose thought there was something fishy about Roger Powel, the Head of Research. I helped her look for proof, while Daisy followed up her own hunch – that Powel's assistant, Sonya Frost, was involved. Frost was a top TV weather presenter until she took the blame when the Bureau failed to forecast a wicked storm. Things got even **more** frosty when Rose told Daisy that her theory was a no-brainer. They fell out big time. Girls!

Turned out they were both kind of right, anyway. Powel **did** have a weather-manipulating machine – but it was Frost's invention, not his. And it was only a harmless prototype. The freaky weather conditions were being caused by a much more powerful model, hidden in the Bureau's basement, which Powel knew nothing about. Sonya had developed it secretly – funded by S.K.U.L. of course – so she could make a historic weather prediction and clear her reputation. She hadn't bargained on the Grand Master having his own plan – to override her machine and keep up the freeze until we entered another ice age.

With Rose's help, Sonya managed to regain control of the machine and get the weather back on track.

GADGET PERFORMANCE NOTES

The calculator code-breaker did a cracking job on the safe in Powel's office.

MISSION RESULT: MISSION ACCOMPLISHED

FELON FACTFILE

NAME: Sonya Frost

ALIASES: None

DETAILS: Highly intelligent – studied physics at Oxford University where her meteorological research made her 'Most Promising Student'. Unfairly sacked from her job as a TV weather presenter to cover up the Weather Bureau's failure to forecast a major storm.

CURRENT STATUS: Released without charge.

COMPILED BY: Agent Millar

CASE NAME: The Power Thief

ASSIGNMENT BRIEFING

Unexplained power cuts had struck across the nation. Even the HQ backup generator was on the blink – poor old Lenny was having to pedal-power the equipment! He wanted us to find out who, or what, was messing with the electricity supply.

ACTION LOG

With the generator playing up, we had to use Blane-power to run Rose's PC and brainpower to search newspapers (**so** yesteryear) for info, instead of the internet. We dug up some interesting articles about the recent theft of two of the three Dark Stones – spooky ancient artefacts supposedly responsible for balancing out Great Britain's power, and said to be capable of plunging Britain back into the Dark Ages if brought together. After M.I.9 had linked us up to an incoming broadcast – a ransom demand from a very nervous-sounding man who claimed to be draining the power – Lenny told Rose to find out who the bumbling bad guy was, and ordered me and

Blane to secure the last Dark Stone. I didn't tell the others, but the third stone actually belonged to my dad. I knew it would be easier to steal it from the high-security Serinturk Museum where it was kept than to try to get through to Daddy at work – he's **impossible** to speak to. Anyway, when we did get the stone, it was a fake – our nervous friend had already taken the real one. We traced his calls to his home address (duh!) and managed to get there just in time to prevent him bringing the stones together. The dreadful threat – a life without hairdryers – was over.

GADGET PERFORMANCE NOTES

My belt-buckle ClimbLine and hairband grappling hook came in very handy when Blane and I had to scale the Serinturk's perimeter wall.

MISSION RESULT: CULPRIT APPREHENDED

FELON FACTFILE

NAME: Brent Gilbert
ALIASES: None
DETAILS: Spent thirty years as a Tour Guide at the Serinturk Museum before being unceremoniously replaced. Mocked for his interest in the Dark Stones.
A reluctant criminal – painfully polite and nervous – who is careful to keep his ransom demand to a reasonable figure.
CURRENT STATUS: Incarcerated

SECTION THREE:
FIT FOR ACTION

COMPILED BY
AGENT BLANE WHITTAKER

'Being a spy is wicked. But it's dangerous too. Sometimes all the brainpower in the world won't get you out of a tight spot – but laying down a few martial arts moves might. To make a top spy, you need to be tough as well as smart. This section gives you some top tips on fitness, combat and stealth – my specialities – for when things get physical.'

ACTIVE AGENT

If you're serious about making it as a spy, you need to chuck away that forged PE excuse letter, dig out your kit from the back of your locker and get yourself training – hard! As Lenny himself found out, when he had to pedal-power the HQ systems during a power cut – at M.I.9, it pays to stay in shape.

INSIDE AND OUT

Regular exercise and a healthy diet are the two key ways to keep yourself in top physical condition. Being active and eating well will boost your energy levels and keep your cardiovascular system – your heart and lungs – in peak condition. And you'll look good too. As Daisy might say, slobby is **so** last season.

SPY DIET

Quality nutrition might seem to clash with school dinners, but even canteen greens will do you good. Make sure you eat at least five portions of fruit and vegetables a day and avoid fatty, sugary or salty foods. Bananas, dried fruit and nuts and seeds are all great snacks for keeping your energy levels up – which as an M.I. High agent, you're gonna need to!

Remember, it is vital to seek expert guidance about the correct nutritional programme and exercise schedule for you. M.I.9 has several qualified Health and Fitness personnel to advise you.

KEEP IT NATURAL

It's good to strive for peak fitness, but don't be tempted to artificially boost your body. Anything that claims to 'improve' your natural abilities is usually pretty dodgy. Performance-enhancing drugs – sometimes used illegally in the ultra-competitive world of professional sport – have damaging side-effects. And when Rose was asked to run tests on the CIA's prototype 'human supercharger' gadget – the MT-3000 – she discovered it was potentially **lethal**. Which made its claim to give you the power of ten men slightly less tempting.

Being fit for action doesn't just mean being particularly strong, or unusually fast, or exceptionally light on your feet – as an M.I.9 operative, you need the whole package. For all-round effectiveness in the field, you'll need to vary your training activities to target different aspects of your physical fitness.

SPEED

If you can clock a decent 100m time, there's a good chance you'll catch your bad guy in a short street chase. Lenny likes to keep tabs on our rapid response time too. Practise short sprints or bursts of speed when you're jogging (or late for registration).

STAMINA

For a more prolonged pursuit, you'll need to work on your stamina. A cross-country run might be your idea of torture, but it'll build up endurance. A stint on a rowing machine is another good option. Mr Flatley's morris-dancing classes don't count.

STRENGTH

An effective punch or block needs muscle power behind it. Resistance training – using gym machines or free weights – is one way to build strength. Exercises that use your body's own weight – like press-ups, squats and lunges – don't need fancy kit and are just as effective.

AGILITY

You never know when you might need to scale a military complex's perimeter wall or jump from one rooftop to the next. We can't all be Spiderman, but a couple of sessions now and then on the M.I.9 climbing wall should keep you agile.

COORDINATION

Playing a ball sport regularly will help you develop the split-second coordination you need for things like weapon evasion. Catching double-agent Chad 'fat-head' Turner came down to instinctive skills I'd picked up playing on the school football team.

FLEXIBILITY

Avoiding the infra-red beams of an anti-intruder system may mean getting seriously bendy. Yoga and Pilates are both great ways to improve your overall flexibility and muscle tone, and also help with breathing. Doing t'ai chi stretches helps me concentrate too – even if Rose and Daisy do take the mickey.

THE ART OF COMBAT

In my experience, saving the day often involves a face-off with some big ugly bruiser. It's vital that you can defend yourself and, if needs be, put an opponent out of action. But basic brawling is scrappy and ineffective. As a spy, you need to develop an ultra-efficient fighting style – in other words, a martial art.

THE TRUE WAY

Since their early history, the Japanese have turned to **bujitsu** – the martial arts – for both their awesome combat potential and their ability to enrich the soul. The '**-do**' of **judo**, **aikido** and **kendo** means the 'way' or 'road' – these arts offer a path to inner balance and harmony, as well as physical supremacy.

To master a martial art, you need to get your head sorted first. Practise emptying your mind of all distracting thoughts. This is one of the key principles of **karate** – my speciality. '**Kara**' actually means 'empty'. Having a fact-packed, hyperactive brain is OK if you have Rose's role, but for combat you need clarity and focus.*

LEARNING THE MOVES

Once you've got the mindset, you need a good **sensei** – an instructor. The teachers

If an empty head helps, Daisy should be a black belt. R.G.

at M.I.9's **dojo** – karate training club – are among the finest in the world. They'll show you the key postures, kicks, punches and blocking moves, and how to channel your strength into your point of contact. Once you've got the basic techniques, practise them over and over, and start working on combinations. You can pick up some cool moves from kung-fu movies too.

BE CREATIVE

When it comes down to the real thing – combat in action – don't be afraid to improvise a little. When I took on Tony Frisco in the school music room, I had to make the best of what I had to hand. It's amazing what you can do with a bass drum and a little imagination.

BEING BACKUP

If fitness and combat skills are among your key strengths, you're likely to be assigned the role of providing backup – keeping a close eye on a fellow agent's mission progress, ready to step in if things get sticky. As martial arts expert of the M.I. High team, I get landed with most of the counter-surveillance, as Lenny calls it. Here are my top tips, so you don't mess up being the backup.

STAY FOCUSED

It only takes a moment to lose contact with your fellow agent. On my very first mission, I lost track of Daisy. I was swatting up on my counter-surveillance theory from one of Lenny's textbooks while on the job. She never let me forget it, of course. So stay close and focused, and avoid any distractions.

BLENDING IN

When you're providing covert support for someone on an assignment, you need to keep a low profile. Practise making the most of any cover that your situation provides. Try to stay out of the open, where you are exposed, by ducking and dodging behind stuff.

Your M.I. High uniform has a hi-tech gel coating that reflects the colours of your immediate surroundings, making it easier to blend in. Looks real smart too.

NEW TECHNOLOGY

Staying out of sight could be about to get a whole lot easier. According to Lenny, the M.I.9 technical guys are working on a SpookSuit that projects on to its surface a digital copy of whatever background you're standing against. Makes you practically invisible. Now that would be well cool.

MISSION FILE 5

ASSIGNMENT BRIEFING

Lenny told us that Britain's anti-missile defence satellite, SPARTA, was about to be replaced. But recent attacks against the UK Space Centre by a computer hacker, calling himself The Worm, had left M.I.9 anxious that the launch of SPARTA's replacement system might be sabotaged – leaving Britain vulnerable to enemy attack. We had to find The Worm and fast.

ACTION LOG

From his nerdy profile and juvenile spelling of 'kaos', we reckoned our suspect was probably young and immature – but nevertheless brilliant enough to be seriously dangerous. Blane managed to chat to him online, through an alternative blogging and gaming site – but not long enough for me to run a trace. The only way I could see to stop him from sabotaging the Space Centre launch was to get someone else inside the Centre's system too, to defend it from The Worm's attack. We needed an expert online-gamer. Blane's best friend, Stewart, was the obvious choice – he's brilliant with computers. According to Blane, he's 'got a thing' for Daisy – why would someone as clever as Stewart fancy **her**?? – so she was able to persuade him to let her go round to his house to play my made-up *Missile Defence* game. Unknown to Stewart, my software linked his home computer to the Space Centre system, and in playing the game, he was unknowingly defending the SPARTA launch program from The Worm's attack. It worked – Stewart narrowly defeated The Worm. The launch went off OK. And the computer-tracking device that Lenny had given Blane locked on to The Worm's online activity, leading Blane straight to the culprit – a nerdy young kid, hacking away from his bedroom PC.

GADGET PERFORMANCE NOTES

Blane's gadget – disguised as a football supporter's key-fob – did its job, picking up The Worm's location from his hacking activity. It was also tastefully created in the colours of his favourite team – Leyton Orient.

MISSION RESULT: OBJECTIVE ACHIEVED

FELON FACTFILE

NAME: Steven Finkle
ALIASES: The Worm
DETAILS: A phenomenally gifted, but excruciatingly geeky, schoolboy – top of his class in everything, except PE – who likes to show off his exceptional IT skills by hacking into and sabotaging official computer systems. His mummy thinks he's an angel.
CURRENT STATUS: Undergoing re-education.

MISSION FILE 6

ASSIGNMENT BRIEFING

Surprised to be briefed not by Lenny but
by a teenage CIA agent called Chad Turner
(who **so** fancied himself). Apparently, our
American counterparts were having problems
with a gadget they'd spent millions of dollars
developing – the MT-3000. It was meant to make
an agent superhuman – ten times as strong and
intelligent. But it had a fault. Rose had till noon
the following day to figure out the bug.

ACTION LOG

My first job was to handle the drop-off of the MT-3000s – by
an undercover CIA courier. Thanks to Ms Templeman, I
messed up – the briefcase got picked up by accident by one of
the staff. Chad was only too happy to use his flashy miniature
X-ray cam to track down the missing case – what a show-off!
Daisy was like 'Oh – you're **so amazing**, Chad!' (barf).

Rose was having a hard time figuring out the fault in the
MT-3000, so I volunteered to put one on – against Lenny's
orders – so she could run some tests. It felt amazing, until I
started having these uncontrollable spasms, like I was doing
a dad-dance or something. Turned out the device made your

COMPILED BY: *Agent Whittaker*
CASE NAME: *Super Blane*

body short-circuit if you kept it on and I couldn't get it off! Rose **just** managed to find a way to remove the dodgy gadget before I went into meltdown.

With Rose having solved the MT-3000 glitch, Chad made to head home stateside with the gadgets. But from a couple of things he'd let slip, Rose had a hunch that he wasn't playing straight. How could he work for the CIA – based in Virginia – when he said he lived in LA? We found proof of his double-dealing on his swanky laptop. He was planning to sell the MT-3000s, and details of our secret set-up, to the Grand Master for a cool $10,000,000! Daisy **finally** realized what a jerk he was, and I used a bit of plain Blane sprint-and-shoot football magic to bring him in.

GADGET PERFORMANCE NOTES

The MT-3000 certainly made me feel superhuman – but only till it almost wiped me out!

MISSION RESULT: DOUBLE-AGENT EXPOSED

FELON FACTFILE
NAME: Chad Turner
ALIASES: ~~None~~ *Superjerk*
DETAILS: Blond-haired, blue-eyed, super-smooth CIA agent – Daisy's all-round dream date. Wears sunglasses indoors and claims to 'eat danger for breakfast'. Exposed as a double-crossing double-agent scheming to sell top-secret CIA gadgets and M.I.9 intelligence to S.K.U.L.
CURRENT STATUS: Incarcerated

SECTION FOUR:
GOING UNDERCOVER

COMPILED BY
AGENT DAISY MILLAR

'Missions often call for close-quarter surveillance of a suspect or infiltration of an organization. Obviously, you can't just go mooching about after somebody, or strolling around private premises, in your official M.I.9 gear (however good you might look in it). A key element of spycraft – and my own area of expertise – is the ability to assume a false identity. It's amazing who will talk to you, and the places you can bluff your way into, if you can create the right phoney persona.'*

* Plus, being the good-at-disguises one means I get to try out different hairstyles and outfits, which is so cool.

The first step in creating a false identity – or a 'legend' as we call it in the trade – is to decide on what character you're going to become and why. For instance, when I needed to get up-close-and-personal with a suspicious political figure – the British PM no less – I posed as a journalist. To infiltrate a military base, you might be able to find a way past security as a cleaner or electrician.

Once you've decided on your cover identity, it's vital that you think your way into your role, so that you can carry it off under extreme pressure.

HISTORY HOMEWORK

Your character needs a full personal history as you never know when you might be asked where you grew up, what your mum's maiden name is or how you got that interesting scar on your forearm. M.I.9 will often decide on an ideal identity for you, and provide you with a full file of background information about the new you. Do your homework, because if you're not familiar enough with your fake background, you're almost certain to be rumbled.

PLANNING A PERSONALITY

To be convincing in a role, you need to give your character depth. Work on the details and quirks of your false persona until it's believably real. Here are a few questions to get you started:

What's your basic personality type? Easy-going? Anxious? Confident? Shy? Nerdy?

What's your body language like? Dynamic and animated? Nervous? Do you slouch? Swagger? Bite your nails? Flick your hair back? Pick your nose?

How do you talk? Fast? Not much? Very loud? With an accent? In broken English?

THE ULTIMATE CHALLENGE

The ultimate challenge for an undercover expert is to impersonate a real individual. If an assignment requires you to stand in for an actual person, you'll need to work doubly hard on all the elements above. Study their background, research their personality and behavioural habits, mimic their body language and voice. You'll also need to look the part, which brings us to our next top-secret topic . . .

DISGUISE – LOOKS ARE EVERYTHING

Once you've developed the phoney role you're going to play to achieve your mission goal, you need to focus on altering your physical appearance to fit the part. Obviously, it's important that you're not recognizable and your looks need to support your fake identity – you won't be convincing with a cleaning-lady cover if you're done up like a film star.

HAIRDOS AND DON'TS

Hair is **so** important. But as a spy, it's **even more** important than for regular people. A fundamental change in your hairstyle will make you instantly less recognizable. You'll have the most options if you're a girl with long hair. But even close-cropped boys can recolour or restyle. Good quality wigs are invaluable as they give you the opportunity to change into your disguise quickly, without damaging your hair. Remember: if you go for a different 'natural' hair colour, don't forget to colour your eyebrows too. If your hair says 'brunette' but your eyebrows say 'blonde', it might blow your cover.

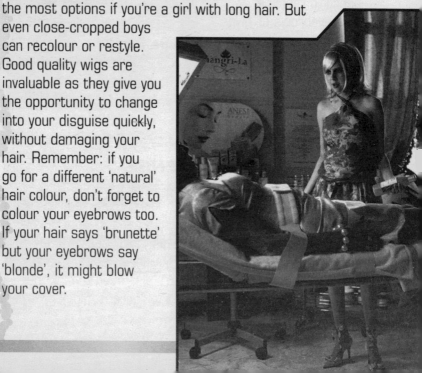

SPECIAL FEATURES

Even with your hair styled differently, your facial features
are likely to give you away. But it's amazing what a quick
makeover can do (as I've tried telling Rose like a **zillion**
times). Here are just a few easy alterations to help you
change face.

❱ Alter your basic skin
tone with foundation,
talc or tan-in-a-bottle.

❱ Use coloured contact
lenses to change your
natural iris colour.

❱ Add a fake beauty spot
or birthmark (or conceal
a real one).

❱ Use an eyebrow
pencil to reshape
your eyebrows or give
yourself frown lines and
crow's feet (urgh!).

❱ Experiment with fake
facial hair (boys).

PROSTHETICS

If make-up isn't radical enough to achieve the degree of
facial disguise your assignment requires, there are more
extreme options. M.I.9 employs a team of prosthetic
specialists. They'll work magic with synthetic skin and hi-
tech modelling material to temporarily add thirty years to
your age or create whatever facial alterations you require.*

---

* No nose jobs or other cosmetic surgical procedures though. I've tried.

DISGUISE – COMPLETING THE ILLUSION

Reinventing your hairstyle and facial features will help make you less recognizable, but to really sell your role, you also need to think about clothing and accessories. Thinking about what to wear on an undercover assignment is all-important and is one of the reasons I love my job.

CLOTHING

Make sure your clothing fits the personality you're trying to project. The M.I.9 Subterfuge Apparel guys will provide you with whatever outfit you need – anything from an Armani business suit to oil-stained denim overalls. Even if you think your character should dress casually, avoid the scruffy, black-everything option.*

HATS AND SPECS

Putting on a hat is an easy way to instantly transform your appearance and a great option to hide a telltale hairstyle. Pick a hat that suits your fake character: a wide-brimmed safari hat if you're posing as a globe-trotting naturalist;

* No particular espionage-related reason – I just **hate** that Goth look.

a beret if you're meant to be an artist;
a trendy woolly hat if you're passing
yourself off as a champion snowboarder.

Spectacles too can alter your image
immediately. The massive variety of
styles means you should be able to
find a pair that conjures up your new
personality. Take care only to use
glasses with blank lenses or ones fitted
with your own prescription – stumbling
around the scene of an investigation with
blurred vision won't do you any favours.

ACCESSORIZE, GUYS

Working undercover, you won't be able to
carry any suspicious equipment with you –
only your fake character's 'ordinary' personal
effects. But a little clever use of specialized
accessories can allow you to carry covert
items without detection:

❭ a walking stick will seem quite natural if you're posing
  as a pensioner – and its hollow centre will nicely
  accommodate that tightly rolled, top-secret blueprint
  that you have been asked to retrieve.
❭ chunky earrings won't look amiss if you're a fashion
  magazine editor and, when unscrewed, are just the place
  to conceal tiny phials of secret sample formulae.

**Think hard about what accessories your character might
reasonably be expected to have and how they might be used
to assist your mission.**

PRE-PREPARED PROFILES

You never know when you may be called upon to go undercover. It's a good idea to develop a number of key phoney profiles, any one of which you can adopt at short notice. Two of my own favourite legends are shown on the next pages.

Prepare a handful of roles, with as wide a range of applications as possible – a scientific boffin persona might get you into a research institution, but how about also having a photographer cover on standby, in case you need to infiltrate the media?

PHONEY PHONECALLS

Sometimes it's only over the telephone that you need to fake a false identity. It's amazing what you can get done if the person on the other end of the phone believes you really **are** their Head Office boss, local MP or a member of the royal family. Practise a variety of phone voices and accents so you can confidently pull off the necessary deception in an emergency.

ALIAS: CHARLOTTE GRAHAM

OCCUPATION: Journalist – reporter for the *United Schools' Gazette*.

CHARACTER: Confident, pushy, go-get-that-front-page-story type.

PERSONAL HISTORY: Parents both work in the media. Had her first article – about her pet guinea pig's escape and dramatic recapture – published when she was only seven. Former co-editor of failed teen-mag *Homework Enthusiast*.

DISGUISE DETAILS: Smart pinstriped trouser suit; narrow black-framed glasses; hair in immaculate black bob (wig); black-and-white neck scarf; clipboard.

ALIAS: MILAN RADISON

OCCUPATION: None – spoilt heiress and party girl.

CHARACTER: Shallow, self-obsessed shopaholic, only interested in her appearance and Daddy's credit card.

PERSONAL HISTORY: Only child of seriously loaded American property magnate. Raised on a ranch in Texas, moved to London when father bought a large chunk of SW7. Emotionally scarred by the traumatic experience of a bad manicure in 2003.

DISGUISE DETAILS: Little pink dress; fur stole (pink); big shades (pink); brooch (pink); strappy high heels (pink); blonde rich-girl hairdo held in Alice band (pink); eavesdropping earrings (cute).

ALIAS:

OCCUPATION:

CHARACTER:

PERSONAL HISTORY:

DISGUISE DETAILS:

ALIAS:

OCCUPATION:

CHARACTER:

PERSONAL HISTORY:

DISGUISE DETAILS:

Use this page to record details of your own favourite false identities.

||||||||||||||||||||||||||||||||||||||||||||||||||||

COMPILED BY: *Agent Whittaker*
CASE NAME: *Spy Animals*

ASSIGNMENT BRIEFING

Lenny dropped a bombshell at the briefing – M.I.9 was shutting us down! He'd been at a meeting with his boss, discussing our operation at St Hope's, when a suspicious transmission had triggered a security alert – someone was bugging their chat. M.I.9 thought the same someone was now closing in on HQ. They wanted us to lay low – suspending us from active duty!

ACTION LOG

Lenny had told us to 'trust no one'. But Daisy and I were still stunned when Rose's suspicious behaviour – not being straight with us and secretly visiting HQ despite having been told it was off-limits – seemed to suggest that **she** might be the bad guy. And Rose wasn't the only one acting strangely. Ms Templeman and Mr Flatley were coming out with all sorts of embarrassing inner secrets – like they couldn't help themselves. We discovered someone was firing off darts containing a truth serum. When Daisy caught one in the arm, she confronted Rose – who explained that under Lenny's orders, she'd been working independently. By now we'd all had enough of 'laying low' – it was back to full team action, whatever M.I.9 said. Rose quickly knocked up an antidote for the truth serum (but not before I'd **almost** got Daisy to admit she fancies me). Rose also came up with a clever 'chemical sniffer' gadget to track the serum's source. It led us to an ice-cream van outside the school gates. The phoney ice-cream man turned out to be our villain – Silas Fenton, a loopy inventor with a flair for equipping animals to do his dirty work. He'd launched the truth serum darts from – get this – a **tortoise**. And he'd saved his most ingenious and dangerous invention till last – a swarm of remote-controlled flies, each fitted with miniature spy-cam contact lenses and carrying a brain-draining microchip! His spy flies backfired, though, when Rose reprogrammed them to target **him** – leaving him totally harmless.

GADGET PERFORMANCE NOTES

I used my badge – a sonic detonator – to set off a blast inside Fenton's ice-cream control van. Wasn't pretty. Raspberry Ripple **everywhere**.

MISSION RESULT: SECURITY THREAT NEUTRALIZED

FELON FACTFILE

NAME: Silas Fenton
ALIASES: None
DETAILS: An unhinged inventor, who desperately wants to be a member of S.K.U.L. To prove his worth to the Grand Master (who thinks he's a liability) attempted to expose the M.I.9 operation at St Hope's. Deployed the G.M.'s beloved rabbit, General Flopsy, as a 'Bionic Bunny' – a living surveillance device.
CURRENT STATUS: Allowed to go free, empty-brained (as detention would expose the accuracy of his suspicions to S.K.U.L.).

COMPILED BY: Agent Millar

CASE NAME: Forever Young

ASSIGNMENT BRIEFING

Lenny had a real puzzle for us. Someone had attacked NOSE
(that's the 'National Organization of Scientific Exploration' –
apparently!). Its team of super-clever government scientists had
somehow been made to regress, and they were behaving like a
bunch of toddlers. Our job was to find out who was responsible
and how to get the victims back to normal.

ACTION LOG

Lenny asked Rose to start by analysing the contents of the NOSE
lab – he'd had it all boxed up and brought to HQ. Blane (**not**
impressed) was told to babysit the toddlerified NOSE boss, Dr
Grabworst, on the off chance that he might offer some clues.
Between them, they figured out that the scientists had been given
contaminated drinking water. The evidence suggested a link with
a beauty clinic called Shangri La. It was time for me to work my
disguise magic – becoming Milan Radison, American heiress – in
order to investigate. Sure enough, I discovered that the woman
running the clinic – a creepy old bat called Vanessa Zeitgeist –
had brewed a 'regression formula' that the Grand Master was
planning to use to cripple key organizations. Unfortunately, she
rumbled me and managed to tie me down. But a little Chinese
self-dislocation and some nifty work with a pair of hairdryers soon
gave me the upper hand. I managed to talk Zeitgeist into giving
us her secret formula. It was a good job too – at St Hope's, the

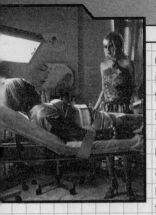

contaminated water sample had found its way into the canteen custard, thanks to the infantile Dr Grabworst. The entire school – pupils **and** staff – had been infected and were behaving like toddlers. Only when Rose had worked out an antidote from the formula, and Blane had managed to use the ventilation system to disperse it, did everyone get back to normal. If you can call any of our staff 'normal'.

GADGET PERFORMANCE NOTES

Rose gave me some great eavesdropping earrings. They worked a treat *and* looked **fabulous**.

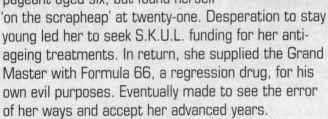

MISSION RESULT:

PLOT
THWARTED

FELON FACTFILE
NAME: Vanessa Zeitgeist
ALIASES: None
DETAILS: Former beauty icon, now in her sixties. Won her first pageant aged six, but found herself 'on the scrapheap' at twenty-one. Desperation to stay young led her to seek S.K.U.L. funding for her anti-ageing treatments. In return, she supplied the Grand Master with Formula 66, a regression drug, for his own evil purposes. Eventually made to see the error of her ways and accept her advanced years.
CURRENT STATUS: Reformed. No longer supports S.K.U.L. activities. Occasional photo shoots for *Scottish Woollens* magazine.

SECTION FIVE:
USEFUL RESOURCES

COMPILED BY LENNY BICKNALL

'This section includes a number of handy resources for the M.I. High operative – from a Morse code key to a glossary of spy jargon. Ah, I remember learning Morse in my own training days. Ginger and I used oil lamps to signal to . . . ahem . . . anyway . . . please familiarize yourself with the documents and commit as much as you can to memory.'

M.I.HIGH

EXIT STRATEGIES

Your Pencil Communicator's alert beacon could flash into life at any time, calling for an urgent response. It's all too likely to happen when you're in the middle of a lesson. Try one of these excuses for a swift classroom exit that won't arouse suspicion.

SUGGESTED EXCUSE	NOTES ON USAGE
I have a fundraising meeting for the Teacher Appreciation Society.	Ought to be received positively.
I have to go to my great aunt's/second cousin's/neighbour's dog's funeral.	Use only once per relative, and not of anyone your teacher might later meet.
I have an appointment with the Nit Nurse/Infectious Diseases Clinic/Verucca Specialist.	Ideal if your assignment requires that your fellow pupils give you a little space.
I've got my Grade 8 morris-dancing exam.	Expect some stick from your classmates.
I left my tuba in the cloakroom.	Obviously only applicable if you **have** a tuba.
I think my school dinner might have disagreed with me.	High plausibility factor.
I'm due at my Anger Management session.	Likely to deter your teacher from objecting.
I have to urgently attend a secret briefing for an intelligence assignment of national importance.	Deliver with a sarcastic smirk.

EQUIPMENT PROPOSAL FORM

EPF/002/078E   Please submit completed specification to the Technical Development Department.

NB This page (only) is photocopiable without handbook self-destruction.

MORSE CODE

This internationally recognized code is fantastically flexible. You can send messages with it in lots of different ways – with a whistle or buzzer, with flashes of your Pencil Communicator's light, via a building's plumbing system (by tapping out messages on a pipe or radiator) or even using eye blinks and winks.

SIGNAL KEY

In Morse, each letter of the alphabet is represented by a combination of short and long signals – shown in the code key below as dots (short) and dashes (long):

A	. –	J	. – – –	S	. . .
B	– . . .	K	– . –	T	–
C	– . – .	L	. – . .	U	. . –
D	– . .	M	– –	V	. . . –
E	.	N	– .	W	. – –
F	. . – .	O	– – –	X	– . . –
G	– – .	P	. – – .	Y	– . – –
H	. . . .	Q	– – . –	Z	– – . .
I	. .	R	. – .		

If you need to send numbers, there are signals for those too:

0	– – – – –	5	. . . . .
1	. – – – –	6	– . . . .
2	. . – – –	7	– – . . .
3	. . . – –	8	– – – . .
4	. . . . –	9	– – – – .

And you can even use punctuation in your Morse messages:

full stop .	. – . – . –	question mark ?	. . – – . .
comma ,	– – . . – –	open brackets (	– . – – .
		close brackets)	– . – – . –

TIMING IS EVERYTHING

However you're signalling your Morse messages, they'll only be understandable if you keep your timing accurate. A dot lasts for a count of one and a dash for a count of three. Leave a gap for a count of three between letters, and a longer one – for a count of seven – between words.

SHORT MORSE

Once you're confident with the basic signals, work on using shortened versions of common phrases – in the same way you use abbreviations in phone text messages:

PHRASE	ABBREVIATION	MORSE
You are	UR	..–/.–.
See you later	CUL	–.–./..–/.–..
Be seeing you	BCNU	–.../–.–./–./..–

There are also a number of special sign-offs, including:

PHRASE	ABBREVIATION	MORSE
Best regards	73	––.../...––
Love and kisses	88	–––../––––..

OOPS!

Finally, if you make a mistake, don't panic! You can tell the receiver to ditch the last word by sending an error signal – eight dots.

PHONETIC ALPHABET

As an M.I. High spy, you'll often need to communicate by radio – most frequently via your Pencil Communicator. When doing so, you should keep your messages short and clear. You may need to clarify certain spellings – perhaps a secret missile launch codeword, or the internet address of a suspect's blog site. There are a number of 'phonetic alphabets' used by radio operators around the world to clarify spellings. The one given below is the NATO standard, employed in international aviation communications and used by all M.I.9 operatives.

A	Alpha	N	November
B	Bravo	O	Oscar
C	Charlie	P	Papa
D	Delta	Q	Quebec
E	Echo	R	Romeo
F	Foxtrot	S	Sierra
G	Golf	T	Tango
H	Hotel	U	Uniform
I	India	V	Victor
J	Juliet	W	Whisky
K	Kilo	X	X-ray
L	Lima	Y	Yankee
M	Mike	Z	Zulu

Using this alphabet, the criminal organization S.K.U.L. becomes Sierra Kilo Uniform Lima. Or the registration of Mr Flatley's old banger – BDM 75S – would be Bravo Delta Mike Seven Five Sierra.

SPY JARGON

In your undercover life in the world of espionage you'll discover a whole new vocabulary of intelligence-related words and phrases. Here's a selection of spy jargon that might come in handy during your M.I. High assignments.

clandestine operation a mission that is intended to remain permanently secret

dead drop (or dead letter box) a secret location where a message or package may be left for a contact to collect

ghost surveillance close and continued undercover surveillance of a particular target

legend a full fake personality profile used by an agent as a cover identity

mole someone who has infiltrated an intelligence service or other secret organization

point when a spy team are following, or 'tailing', someone, the 'point' is the member of the surveillance team in the closest position to the target

rabbit a target under surveillance

spy dust a chemical substance used to secretly mark someone so that their movements can be traced

‖‖‖‖‖‖‖‖‖‖‖‖‖‖‖‖‖‖‖‖‖‖‖‖‖‖‖

COMPILED BY: Agent Millar
CASE NAME: Red Button Rampage

ASSIGNMENT BRIEFING

M.I.9 wanted us to look after Dylan Towzer, a teenage 'genius' whose amazing inventions had made him the eighth richest kid in the world. OK – he was pretty smart as he'd built a Remote Missile Disarmer and was due to showcase it in an important test demonstration. M.I.9 had got wind of a plot to kidnap him before the test and wanted us to keep an eye on him. Clever **and** rich – I was like 'If I **must**!'

ACTION LOG

Dylan's security was being overseen by General Ryan Scarp. Blane was a **big** fan – he'd read Scarp's SAS memoirs (**how** sad is that?). Scarp had arranged for the army to keep Dylan safe at St Hope's until the demonstration, under the pretence of the school holding an 'Army Week'. My job was to stick close to Dylan – which meant that when he got knocked out by nerve gas in the boys' toilets and spirited away to a secret location, so did I. Our kidnapper turned out to be Scarp himself! He was convinced that the world peace which Dylan's Disarmer would secure would spell an end to the army – something he wasn't going to allow. He smashed up the Disarmer and told us how he was going to hijack the missile demonstration to start a third world war – to keep the army 'in business'. **Total** fruitcake.

It all got pretty hectic after that. We managed to escape while Scarp was elsewhere, giving Dylan the chance to quickly put together a replacement Disarmer. When Scarp returned, we pretended to be captive again, so we could wait for the right moment to foil his deadly plan. By the time he'd set it in action – gaining access to the famous 'red button' under the pretence of running the Disarmer demonstration, then launching live missiles at all the major cities in the world – Blaine and Rose had shown up too. While they helped put Scarp out of action, Dylan used the replacement Disarmer to deactivate the missiles – just in time! The global threat was over and I didn't have to put up with any more sarcastic remarks from mister wise guy Towzer – hurrah!

GADGET PERFORMANCE NOTES
My in-shoe tracking device proved less than ideal – the kidnappers removed my footwear!

MISSION RESULT: CONFLICT AVERTED

FELON FACTFILE
NAME: General Ryan Scarp
ALIASES: None
DETAILS: Deranged British army officer, well-known for his best-selling SAS memoirs. Fanatically pro-army. Considers world peace to represent a threat to the army's continued usefulness and strives to bring about global conflict instead. Claims to have once dug an escape tunnel with a pen.
CURRENT STATUS: Incarcerated

COMPILED BY: *Agent Gupta*

CASE NAME: *The Fugitive*

ASSIGNMENT BRIEFING

Blane's friend Stewart was convinced he'd seen a UFO crash-land. According to Lenny, an 'unmanned space probe' really **had** come down nearby – but he said it was the creation of a foreign power, not aliens. He wanted us to find and secure the crash site, until Air One – a crack M.I.9 special unit – arrived to take over.

ACTION LOG

Blane headed off to search the school grounds, and Daisy and I went to look further afield – but not before I'd overheard Lenny receive a mysterious, top-secret communiqué about 'Project ASD3'. He was very shifty about it. Not like Lenny.

Daisy and I found the crashed probe in the park near school. But Blane had found something even **more** interesting, and radioed us to come see. He'd discovered footprints of green petrochemical slime leading to the school gym. The probe wasn't unmanned after all. The footprints belonged to its human pilot, a boy called Lu, who had been cruelly genetically engineered to withstand the intolerable G-forces that the craft's speed generated. Lu was Project ASD3.

The Air One team, led by this hot-shot former student of Lenny's called Carla Terrini, were bent on finding Lu and 'examining' him – and Lenny seemed to be on their side! But

when they captured Lu and were poised to operate on him, Lenny came good. He hijacked the Air One mobile experimental station – a van – with Lu, Daisy and Blane in it. He'd only been playing along with Air One to see what their intentions were.

By now I'd repaired the damaged space probe with a dimensional stabilizer I'd knocked up in science class. The others joined me – just in time for Lu to make his getaway before Terrini and her goons could stop him. I was glad that Lu was safe, but sorry to see him go – which of course Daisy saw as grounds to call him my **boyfriend**. Arrrgghh – she can be **so** infuriating!

GADGET PERFORMANCE NOTES

The traffic-cone force-field pods that Lenny gave us to create an invisible barrier around the probe did a great job of holding up Air One.

MISSION RESULT: MISSION ACCOMPLISHED

MISSION FILE SUBMISSIONS

On completion of an assignment, it is standard procedure to submit a Mission File report. When writing a report, please follow the format of those included in this handbook. Keep non-essential, subjective comments about your fellow M.I. High team members – 'she so fancies so-and-so', 'he messed up **big** time', 'you wouldn't believe what she was wearing', etc. – to a minimum.

M.I.9 Head Office welcomes all feedback from its agents in the field. If you have any comments regarding this handbook, please don't hesitate to contact us. However, be aware that for security reasons all postal communications addressed to 'The Head of M.I.9' are subjected to rigorous safety testing – scanned for traces of explosives, dunked in a neutralizing chemical bath to deactivate possible toxins and fed through a titanium crushing device to disable any mechanical booby-traps. So it's probably best to email – you just need to flex your super-sleuthing skills to find out the correct address.

For more information on S.K.U.L.'s suspected activities in your local area, make contact with your regional M.I.9 operative – that old lady with the Yorkshire terrier and an eye-patch who's always feeding the ducks. You never know what diabolical scheme the Grand Master may be formulating right under your very nose . . .

You may like to find out more at the following websites:
bbc.co.uk/cbbc/mihigh
mi5.gov.uk
mi6.gov.uk/output/Page79.html